Mater

Disney PRESS
New York • Los Angeles

Mater has many feelings.

Mater cries.
He cries when he is sad.

Mater laughs.
He laughs when he is happy.

Mater frowns.
He frowns when he is angry.

Mater shakes.
He shakes when he is scared.

Mater yawns.
He yawns when he is tired.

Shhhh!